Defoe Abbott Marx Hardy Machiavelli Montaigne Chesterton Cooper Emerson Joyce Austen Hugo Eliot Grimm
Melville Carroll Christie Haggard Molière
Stoker Maupassant Byron Schiller
Wilde Garnett Einstein Fitzgerald Engels Smith Kafka
Goethe Hawthorne Hall
Cotton Dostoyevsky Willis
Baum Henry Kipling Doyle
Leslie Dumas Flaubert Turgenev Nietzsche Balzac
Stockton Vatsyayana Crane
Burroughs Verne
Curtis Tocqueville Whitman Gogol Vinci
Homer Widger Tolstoy Busch
Darwin Thoreau Twain
Potter Freud Zola Scott
Kant Jowett Stevenson Dickens Plato Harte
Andersen Burton Hesse
London Descartes Cervantes
Poe Aristotle Voltaire Cooke
Hale James Hastings
Bunner Shakespeare Irving
Richter Chambers
Doré Dante Chekhov da Shaw Wodehouse Benedict Alcott
Swift Pushkin
Newton

tredition

tredition was established in 2006 by Sandra Latusseck and Soenke Schulz. Based in Hamburg, Germany, tredition offers publishing solutions to authors and publishing houses, combined with worldwide distribution of printed and digital book content. tredition is uniquely positioned to enable authors and publishing houses to create books on their own terms and without conventional manufacturing risks.

For more information please visit: www.tredition.com

TREDITION CLASSICS

This book is part of the TREDITION CLASSICS series. The creators of this series are united by passion for literature and driven by the intention of making all public domain books available in printed format again - worldwide. Most TREDITION CLASSICS titles have been out of print and off the bookstore shelves for decades. At tredition we believe that a great book never goes out of style and that its value is eternal. Several mostly non-profit literature projects provide content to tredition. To support their good work, tredition donates a portion of the proceeds from each sold copy. As a reader of a TREDITION CLASSICS book, you support our mission to save many of the amazing works of world literature from oblivion. See all available books at www.tredition.com.

Project Gutenberg

The content for this book has been graciously provided by Project Gutenberg. Project Gutenberg is a non-profit organization founded by Michael Hart in 1971 at the University of Illinois. The mission of Project Gutenberg is simple: To encourage the creation and distribution of eBooks. Project Gutenberg is the first and largest collection of public domain eBooks.

The Rose-Jar

Thomas S. (Thomas Samuel) Jones

Imprint

This book is part of TREDITION CLASSICS

Author: Thomas S. (Thomas Samuel) Jones
Cover design: Buchgut, Berlin – Germany

Publisher: tredition GmbH, Hamburg - Germany
ISBN: 978-3-8472-1500-4

www.tredition.com
www.tredition.de

Copyright:
The content of this book is sourced from the public domain.

The intention of the TREDITION CLASSICS series is to make world literature in the public domain available in printed format. Literary enthusiasts and organizations, such as Project Gutenberg, worldwide have scanned and digitally edited the original texts. tredition has subsequently formatted and redesigned the content into a modern reading layout. Therefore, we cannot guarantee the exact reproduction of the original format of a particular historic edition. Please also note that no modifications have been made to the spelling, therefore it may differ from the orthography used today.

The Rose-Jar

Thomas S. Jones, Jr.

Author of *The Path o' Dreams*, etc.

Clinton, New York

GEORGE WILLIAM BROWNING

The author desires to thank the editors of Appleton's Magazine, Everybody's Magazine, Lippincott's Magazine, The New York Times, The Smart Set, and the other publications in which the verses in this collection originally appeared, for their kind permission to reprint.

This Edition of *The Rose-Jar* Printed by George William Browning at Clinton New York during the Summer of 1906 consists of Three Hundred copies on Deckle-Edged Paper, with Twelve additional copies on Imperial Japan Vellum (Insetsu Kioku).

NUMBER 258

To the Memory of My Mother

As in a Rose-Jar

As in a rose-jar filled with petals sweet

Blown long ago in some old garden place,

Mayhap, where you and I, a little space,

Drank deep of love and knew that love was fleet —

Or leaves once gathered from a lost retreat

By one who never will again retrace

Her silent footsteps — one, whose gentle face

Was fairer than the roses at her feet;

So, deep within the vase of memory,

I keep my dust of roses fresh and dear

As in the days before I knew the smart

Of time and death. Nor aught can take from me

The haunting fragrance that still lingers here —

As in a rose-jar, so within my heart!

The Island

There is an island in the silent sea,

Whose marge the wistful waves lap listlessly —

An isle of rest for those who used to be.

For ne'er an echo wakes that towering wall,

Whose blackened crags answer none other call

Save the lone ocean's rhythmic rise and fall.

Only the song the sea sings as she laves

That sleep-bound shore with sad caressing waves,

The while the dead sleep sweeter in their graves.

'Tis oh! so still they sleep within each tomb,

Cool in long shadows of the cypress gloom,

Breathing in death the moon-flower's rank perfume.

They know not when slow barges on the mere

Enter the portals of that place austere —

Enter and so forever disappear!

And in this island of a silent sea,

Whose marge e'er wistful waves lap listlessly,

Is rest, — is peace for all eternity.

You and I

Over the hills where the pine-trees grow,

With a laugh to answer the wind at play.

Why do I laugh? I do not know,

But you and I once passed this way.

Down in the hollow now white with snow

My heart is singing a song today.

Why do I sing? I do not know,

But you and I were here in May.

A Ballade of Old Romance

When April spreads her mantle green
Across the pasture-lands of snow,
And Spring's first scarlet breasts are seen
Where treetops rustle to and fro;
Then come fair fragrant dreams as though
Our lightest fancy to entrance
And paint us what we fain would know
Adown the lanes of Old Romance.

Anon, we see the golden sheen
Of burnished mail the sunbeams throw,
Flashing the poplars tall between,
As knights ride by to meet the foe;
Or, mayhap, shepherd lads who blow
On slender pipes, a pastoral dance —
Ah, strong were they in weal and woe
Adown the lanes of Old Romance!

But now the vast years intervene,
The fountain long has ceased its flow,
And silence rules the lone demesne
That once held such a goodly show;
Yet time, at least, does this bestow
Nor leave the best to fleeting chance —
They live again in fancy's glow
Adown the lanes of Old Romance.

ENVOY

Sweet, still for us some blossoms grow

From out that dim and dear expanse—
Come, take my hand and we shall go
Adown the lanes of Old Romance!

A Voice From the Far Away

I heard a voice from the far away

Softly say this to me—

"You will find the heart of the world some day

And the why of the things that be;

You will see the grief of the yea and nay

And the price of frailty.

"And upon your lute you will weave a theme

Which the world will harken and know;

For every note of the song will teem

With a great soul's overflow—

You will speak the meaning within a dream

And the pain in the afterglow.

"But for all of this there's a price—

'Tis the price of minstrelsy—

You will never have of the things you play,

Sad singer of poetry,

And throughout your life you will go for aye,

Heart-hungry and silently!"

I heard a voice from the far away

Softly say this to me.

April

Throughout the vale again Narcissus cries
And Echo answers from her dark retreat,
While Zephyr heavy-laden with the sweet,
Fresh scent of blooms across the pasture hies;
Above, the blueness of the April skies,
Matched by the lure unto the wandering feet
That e'er must go ere Spring could be complete
To the green wood where laughing Eros lies.
O April lover, hear the pipes that call,
The pipes of Pan a-blowing lustily,
They call to you and me, and he who hears
Must ever after be Young April's thrall—
So, faring thus together, we shall see
The Islands of the Blest between the Spheres!

A Yesterday

I held you in my arms — so happy I,
Who quite forgot the while that moments fly;
Nor ever dreamed that they could pass away,
Till it was yesterday.
Yet, just because that hour was long ago
And seems to me so near — well, this I know
That sometime I shall clasp your hand and say:
Was there a yesterday?

Violets

'Twas just at sundown, when the leaves were wet
With evening dew,
Far in the fields where sky and violet
Blend rifts of blue—
But for a moment, deep among the flowers
And rain-sweet grass,
I saw her—loved her—and as April showers
Beheld her pass.
O, the lone vastness of the afterglow,
Unknown before;
Shall e'er I see that face where violets grow,
Perchance, once more!
Yet no one comes save night, with wild regrets
And silent pain—
Only sometimes the scent of violets
On wind-blown rain.

A Song of Life

What if the song is sung, I say,
As long as the song was sung!
Did we not meet with the blood's best play
The lash of the winds and the rain that stung,
And the tang of the salty spray?
Did we not drink the last drop that clung
To the golden bowl with its glowing fire,
Yet so cool to our burning tongue?
Did we not love with a love entire
That made up for all and a world of clay
In a moment of wild desire?
What if the song is sung, I say,
As long as the song was sung!

As a Still Brook

As a still brook within the woodland's green
Sings softly to itself the live-long day,
Unconscious of its gentle roundelay,
Its open purity and silver sheen —
Knowing not how in all that wild demesne,
Its music is a strain the angels play
And its fair face a jewel amid the gray,
Beshadowed places that it flows between;
So your dear love, a simple forest stream,
Bearing the wealth of all that life can hold, —
Nor ever dreaming of the worth that lies
Deep in your heart — why, you have made it seem
That every empty hour is wrought of gold
And this tear-sodden world, a Paradise!

At the Window

I looked out of my window tall
And laughed to see the May,
For everything both great and small
Was on a holiday.
Then Love came by and laughed at me,
And I forgot the Spring —
Only I knew the ecstasy
Of madly listening.
And now the branches all again
Are red with vernal May,
But tears have dimmed the window-pane —
And no one comes my way.

A Sea Spell

The sunset sea—a goblet thick inlaid
With jewels wrought in golden filigree,
An opal from some elfin treasury
Burning with fire and flashing every shade;
While round the dim horizon, wide displayed
The clouds pile up their largess tenderly
As if to clothe the beauty of the sea
In filmy gossamer and soft brocade.
And far away I think I almost hear
A horn's faint echo through the dusk-hour's veil
As in the happy, golden days of yore—
Mayhap, e'en now upon this magic mere
Frail shallops will flit by and mermaids pale
Will lure us back to fairy-land once more!

The Silent Country

Wave, wave sweet blooms of May and on your wings

Bear me away with drowsy winnowings

To some far twilight land where steals a stream

From out the cool and soundless groves of Dream.

For in the Spring is such a bitter smart

Even the thought of it will break my heart,

So take me softly to a leafy bed

Where I shall dream and dream you are not dead!

The Sport of a God

Though they say Jove laughs at the lover's vow —
At the lover's vow that must break some day —
Still we smiled as we loved in a distant May
When the blooms were heavy upon the bough.
O, the mocking difference of then and now!
It isn't a thought that will make one gay,
Though they say Jove laughs at the lover's vow —
At the lover's vow that must break some day.
Yet, perhaps, the god knows the best way how
To carry a mask when the feet are clay;
So I too shall laugh at the merry play,
For down in his heart there's a knife, I trow,
Though they say Jove laughs at the lover's vow.

Remembrance

Sweet rosemary within the lane
The while the day is warm and clear,
And ne'er a thought of bitter rain
Or the road-side sere.
But there are flowers more dear to me
That time can never set apart—
The fragrant blooms of memory
That grow within the heart.

In Days of Old

Of all the ages' gain, the ages' loss,

A wealth of wonders and so much away —

When now hears one the woodland elves at play,

Or angry dryads where tall tree-tops toss.

No more they lightly tread the dewy moss

As danced they through cool haunts in ecstasy;

But rank and lost the paths in lone decay

Where fairy footsteps once were wont to cross.

O, happy Greeks, who knew the gods so well,

To you I burn my sacrificial fire!

Again reveal the mystic hidden rune

Whereby to find the slopes of asphodel —

Ah, then to hear Apollo charm his lyre

And see Diana 'neath the sickle moon.

We Once Built a House o' Dreams

We once built a house o' dreams
At the break o' day
Made from out the first gold beams
On the sward astray.
Little did we think or care
'Twas not safe nor strong;
We were very happy there
And the day was long.
Now we leave our house o' dreams,
Why, we do not know;
Only this — so strange it seems
And so hard to go!

A Song of the Way

Give me the road, the great broad road,

That wanders over the hill;

Give me a heart without a care

And a free, unfettered will—

Ah, thus to journey, thus to fare,

With only the skies to frown,

And happy I, if the ways but lie

Away, away from the town.

Give me the path, the wild-wood path

That wanders deep in a dell,

Where silence sleeps and sunbeams fain

Would waken the slumber spell—

For there the gods find the world again,

Immortals of ancient lore,

And time is gone, and a mad-glad faun

Knows the glades of Greece once more.

In Trinity Church-Yard at Sunset

How still they sleep within the city moil
In their old church-yard with its sighing trees,
Where sometimes through the din a twilight breeze
Makes one forget the busy streets of toil;
But they have little thought of worldly spoil
Or the great gain of mortal victories,
Their hopes, their dreams, are cold and dead as these
Quaint, time-worn gravestones crumbling on the soil.
Yet they once lived and struggled years ago;
Their hearts beat madly as these hearts of ours—
And now is all undone in dreamless rest?
See, a great city stands against the glow—
Their city, they who here beneath the flowers
Have known so long God's gift of peace, most blest!

Where Cross-Roads Part

Glad roads of Spring — O lanes of laughing May

As fleeting as the shadow-clouds at play

With sunbeams rife upon the grassy green;

O golden lanes — through roads that lie between

Amid what darkened sweep lost I the way?

Or was't the stripling Youth, whose roundelay

Awoke the echoes of the throbbing day

And changed to gladness all the world's dull mien,

Glad roads of Spring?

Apart I stand, distraught with lone dismay,

No more Youth's gladsome biddings to obey,

No more with him Love's strewings lost to glean;

The hills of years now ever intervene,

And bid me say good-bye to you for aye,

Glad roads of Spring!

Saida

We passed along the high-road, you and I,
Though I remember not the place nor when;
Only the wonder of your face, and then
That you passed by.
But that was long ago, and I forget;
Perhaps 'twere better that I went alone,
You might not e'er have loved me had you known,
And yet, and yet—

In Arcady

Although 'tis but a memory,
Still in the days of long ago
We tended sheep in Arcady.
Then were we both of fancy free
And laughing Youth had much to show,
Although 'tis but a memory.
Again the pasture lands we see
Where in the golden summer glow
We tended sheep in Arcady.
And hear the tender harmony
Of shepherd pipes that softly blow,
Although 'tis but a memory.
Nor thought of any end had we
As through the grasses to and fro
We tended sheep in Arcady.
So, what if life now empty be,
Of all the past this do we know,
Although 'tis but a memory,
We tended sheep in Arcady!

The Summer Rain

As one who listens to the summer rain
Against the roof when all the night is still,
Save for the wind beneath the window-sill,
Crooning its homely, comforting refrain, —
And listening feels that neither joy nor pain
Can trouble now — only the faint sweet thrill
Of drowsiness and peace and rest until
The barque glides softly into sleep's domain;
So I, whose empty way leads wandering
Between high garden-walls that hide the sun,
Hear sometimes on the breeze a simple strain
Of an old song you once were wont to sing —
And then forgetting all, I seem as one
Who listens spell-bound to the summer rain.

Impression

A little stone o'ercrept with moss,
And red wild roses flaunting by,
A wistful breeze that seems to sigh
Where the tall grasses toss.
To sigh for one who went away,
Thus it is writ upon the stone —
Nothing can ever make atone
And tears shall fall for aye.
Oh, irony of human vow,
Even the stone is crumbling too,
And tears, — none save the evening dew,
For who remembers now?

Derelicts

A year, a year, and then to miss

That which was all in all for aye;

O Love as fleeting as your kiss,

O Love forever and a day,

To this.

How such a change in one short year,

I cannot, cannot understand;

Oh, why to cast upon Love's bier,

Whose name was written in the sand,

This tear?

Why, when the fields were red with May

When you and I together swore;

Is May so very far away,

Was all so different then, before

Today?

 And did the gods above then smile

When we believed that love would last,

Counting its heart-beats on the dial

Of hours that have too soon slipped past,

The while.

Two boats upon a sea of glass—

A little strength, a little trust;

Yet let the hand of Fate but pass,

Could they withstand the storm-cloud's gust,

Alas!

So, though not knowing, yet must I

Forget one day and feel no more
Your love, which dreamed not e'er to die.
Thank God for that—I close my door.
Good-bye.

The End of the Day

The day is done and every hour is spent
And now it lies a-dying in the west,
Yet with what wonder those last moments blest
Crown all with the chaste kiss of sweet content;
For nature's minstrels sing a carol pent
With the soft music of the spheres suppressed
In one great strain—the while upon night's breast
The dying day sinks down in languishment.
And in those last faint breaths as 'twere in sooth
The halo of some saint, a glowing light
Of purest gold streams through the darkened sky,
A light more wondrous than the dawn of youth—
For 'tis a flame cleft out the veil of night
From that eternal dawn that ne'er can die!

Tristesse

If you were not away

These trees, this south-wind and this dreary day

Would all be mad with joyous ecstasy;

But you are gone, so mourning they with me

Find bitter-sweet in idle fantasy.

How glad, how mad, how gay,

If you were not away!

Interlude

Sometimes from out the rush of pulsing days,

These days whose poetry was lost in prose

So long ago, left desolate on those

Far childhood paths—yet, sometimes from the haze

Of half-forgotten years, fall on our ways

Now drear, a strain of song, a June-blown rose.

Ah, sweet, so sweet unto a heart that knows

The memory of once-remembered Mays!

Only a moment's interlude, and yet

How the heart quaffs the draught that thrills and thrills

Its soul, finding again youth's mysteries.

What matter if tomorrow we forget—

Today the stillness of the sun-lit hills

And the low drowsy hum of summer bees!

To You, Dear Heart

To you, dear heart, whom I have never known
I sing my little songs all wonderingly
That sometime you may hear,—the sweet atone
For all the years and years of search alone—
That sometime you may hear and come to me.
So on I go a-singing down my way
With ne'er a thought of all the journey past,
For this I know—that on one perfect day
When everything is, oh, so glad and gay,
You'll hear and come and claim your own, at last.

Twilight

When twilight falls and all the land is still,
The purple shadows steal across the hill,
And one lone star above a pine-tree's crest
Shines ever brighter, while from out its nest
There breaks the low cry of the whip-poor-will.
And softly grows the ladened hush until
E'en winds list o'er the fields of daffodil
They all day wafted, — 'tis so sweet to rest
When twilight falls.
Let not one drop of this rare nectar spill,
But with the beryl wine your goblet fill.
Drink with me, Love, the golden of the west,
For all is made for love and love is best, —
And, oh, the wonder of the moment's thrill
When twilight falls!

The Poet

For one great Queen who sits in majesty,
Untouched, austere, upon a golden throne,
The like whose loveliness was never known
Of ebony and rose and ivory, —
For her you weave a broidered tapestry,
Rife with rich stains of every color-tone
Inwrought; while she immovable as stone
But watches pitiless and silently.
Yet, should this Queen of Beauty lift her arm
And take your broidered web, — ah, then the prize,
The vast reward of all the scars and shame,
For in the moment as a mystic charm
The cloth is changed to porphyry, and lies
Forever on her breast a frozen flame!

The Hunchback

He never knew the golden thrall of youth,
The ringing step, the rumpled wind-tossed hair,
The reckless laugh untouched of pain or ruth,—
Youth without pity and without a care.
Not his the swift lithe strength that ever slays,
And in its joyous slaying doubly sweet,
Like some young god adown immortal ways,
Crushing the blossoms 'neath unheeding feet.
A twisted back, a face year-scarred and grim,
A very mockery to love's caress,
These were the only birthright given him,—
What should he know, except of ugliness?
But in his fettered heart in longing pent
A wealth of tenderness and, stranger too,
Youth full of pity,—ah, the wonderment,—
He never knew, and yet how well he knew!

The Little Ghosts

Where are they gone, and do you know
If they come back at fall o' dew,
The little ghosts of long ago,
That long ago were you?
And all the songs that ne'er were sung,
And all the dreams that ne'er came true,
Like little children dying young, —
Do they come back to you?

I Know a Quiet Vale

I know a quiet vale where faint winds blow

The silver poplar branches all awry,

And ne'er another sound comes drifting by

Save where the stream's cool waters softly flow;

Wild roses riot there and violets throw

Their perfume recklessly, the while on high

Great snowy clouds pillow the smiling sky

And cast frail shadows on the grass below.

All is the same, the summer stillness dreams

In idleness across the sunny leas,

Until for very drowsiness it seems

The wind has gone to sleep within the trees—

Yet we once laughed at what the years might bring,

And now I am alone, remembering.

Song

Blurred is the moon in a yellow stain,

And the clouds are flying before the wind,

The leaves fall fast in a ghostly rain, —

Summer is left behind.

And left behind the long nights of June,

When the lights were soft in the waters' shine —

Softer your lips when they first met mine —

Blurred is the Autumn moon.

Blurred is the moon in a yellow stain,

And oh, for the warmth of your arms again!

Immutability

Within your hands you hold the wealth of years,
Old Time, — yes, all the gold of yesterday,
All of love's sunshine and the bitter gray
Of tears — oh, the great multitude of tears;
For everything is yours within the spheres
To give or take, or break, or keep for aye,
Nor heed you e'en one wild cry of dismay,
But gather on until all disappears.
Yet love is sweet and we are not so old,
Nor did the gods mean us to separate.
O Time you cannot take my love from me,
Life has so much, so very much to hold
For each, — I must not dream it is too late
And that we'll dwell no more in Arcady.

In the Fall o' Year

I went back an old-time lane
In the fall o' year,
There was wind and bitter rain
And the leaves were sere.
Once the birds were lilting high
In a far-off May —
I remember, you and I
Were as glad as they.
But the branches now are bare
And the lad you knew,
Long ago was buried there —
Long ago with you!

Love's Song

If I had never known

How far would I have wandered wistfully alone,

Hearing no echo of that wondrous song

Whose music lingers long.

Beside whose sweetness pale

Even the soft notes of the nightingale,

Whose theme is wrought of laughter and of tears

From all the deathless years.

Ah, better thus by far

To once have felt the barriers unbar,

And known the moment in a rapt surprise

The song of Paradise!

The Golden Hour

The winds may blow, the sleet may dash the pane
And all our lonely road be clothed in gray,
Yet what care we how dark may be the way,
Or whether e'er we see the sun again;
On shall we journey through the stinging rain,
Our glad hearts beating to a roundelay
Learned long ago in one great, joyous day,
When we first knew we had not lived in vain.
We two have lived, we drank the ruddy wine
And felt the wonder of its burning kiss—
Let come what may there is no earthly power
Can take away that rapture, yours and mine.
Others may weep, who would give all for this,
To find what we have found—the golden hour!

The Dream-Way

It did not look so far, and yet, and yet,

The moments were so easy to forget,

For now without your hand to guide, it seems

I seek in vain to find a way of dreams.

A moon-lit path between aspiring trees,

'Neath wind-blown leaves rustling in harmonies,

A little song that I may never sing —

But oh, the wondrous memory lingering.

And though I never may return until

I clasp your hand beyond these years, why still

There is one guide the path of life along —

A fleeting end of dream-remembered song.

The Spirit of Autumn

Where the winds low list and the leafless trees
Stand gaunt and gray 'gainst the sullen sky,
The naked boughs whisper melodies
Of Summer spent and of Spring gone by—
Of days once glad that are gone forever,
Of lips once true that will answer never,
Of life and love that are but as these
Dead leaves of Autumn grown withered and dry.
But a spirit haunts in the moon's pale glow
And all is changed as she sings a strain,
While the night winds hearken and lightly blow
Her loose-bound hair in a raven-rain—
And bear her song to the distant closes,
Where many a longing heart reposes,
Waking old love-dreams that overflow
In a rapturous joy and wistful pain.
Ah, that song 'tis sweet as the pipes of Pan,
Or faint lutes sounding in Arcady
Through the purple dawn,—yea, far sweeter than
The music that wafts from a Southern sea!
Beneath its spell the wastes bloom in flowers,
And back again come the vanished hours,
For she who sings to the soul of man
Is the Autumn spirit of memory.

On The Long Road

Ah, many were they then of yesterday,

Who bore me gifts of attar and of myrrh,

And leaves of roses delicate that were

Sprung from a garden-close in far Cathay;

While I, unheeding, let them pass their way

Nor cared for all the gifts they might confer,

Watching in vain for one dear loiterer,

Who never dreamed adown my path to stray.

And now out in the lonely road I stand,

Where echoes drearily the ceaseless tread

Of stranger footsteps, slow and burdensome —

I am forgot and empty is each hand,

Save for the dust of roses witherèd,

Yet still I wait for you who never come.

A Postlude

If only in your life to live, might I
Perchance those broken chords with my own meet,
Though quite imperfect, yet but thus to try
Were oh, so wondrous sweet.
Not the broad high-roads which you would have trod,
A lonely wanderer these may not essay,
Still, spirit mine, the by-paths that I plod
Do lead the selfsame way.
And if a little part I should fulfil
Of those fair deeds which you hoped to pursue—
Oh, how content to walk the miles until
I reach my home and you.

An Old Song

Low blowing winds from out a midnight sky,

The falling embers and a kettle's croon—

These three, but oh what sweeter lullaby

Ever awoke beneath the winter's moon.

We know of none the sweeter, you and I,

And oft we've heard together that old tune—

Low blowing winds from out a midnight sky,

The falling embers and a kettle's croon.

Old Roses

Spirit of old-time roses, when the glow
Of eventide steals softly through the trees
Like rosy petals falling, and the breeze
Grows hushed until it sings a love-song, low
And sweet and tender, then I seem to know
You too are somewhere near and watching these
Last wondrous sights of day — God's mysteries
We used to watch together long ago.
And, like a benediction, happiness
Fills all my soul, as if a wandering breath
From that high heaven had wafted down to me —
As if I felt again your dear caress
And knew you to be waiting e'er in death,
Crowned with the roses of eternity.